JER Moncur
Moncure, Jane Belk,
My "w" sound box /
$14.21   on1042476446

3 4028 09469 6508
HARRIS COUNTY PUBLIC LIBRARY

W9-CLR-946

My "w" Sound Box®

WRITTEN BY JANE BELK MONCURE • ILLUSTRATED BY REBECCA THORNBURGH

The Child's World®
childsworld.com

Published by The Child's World®
1980 Lookout Drive • Mankato, MN 56003-1705
800-599-READ • www.childsworld.com

Copyright ©2019 by The Child's World®
All rights reserved. No part of the book may be reproduced or
utilized in any form or by any means without written permission
from the publisher.

ISBN HARDCOVER: 9781503823266
ISBN PAPERBACK: 9781503831483
LCCN: 2017960388

Printed in the United States of America
PA02371

A NOTE TO PARENTS AND EDUCATORS:

Magic moon machines and five fat frogs are just a few of the fun things you can share with children by reading books with them. Reading aloud helps children in so many ways! It introduces them to new words, motivates them to develop their own reading skills, and expands their attention span and listening abilities. So it's important to find time each day to share a book or two . . . or three!

As you read with young children, you can help develop their understanding of how print works by talking about the parts of the book—the cover, the title, the illustrations, and the words that tell the story. As you read, use your finger to point to each word, modeling a gentle sweep from left to right.

Simple word games help develop important prereading skills, including an understanding of rhyme and alliteration (when words share the same beginning sound, such as "six" and "sand"). Try playing with words from a book you've just shared: "What other words start with the same sound as moon?" "Cat and hat, do those words rhyme?" The possibilities are endless—and so are the rewards!

My "w" Sound Box®

Little  had a box. "I will find things

that begin with my **W** sound," she said.

"I will put them into my sound box."

Little  went for a walk in the woods.

She found woodpeckers and a woodchuck.

Did she put them into her box? She did.

Little  looked under some wood chips.

She found lots of wiggly worms.

"In you go," she said.

Little  walked to a well in the woods.

She saw some water in the well.

"This may be a wishing well," she said. She looked all around the well.

Guess what she found? A wand! Little

waved the wand and made a wish. "I wish I

could find more things for my box," she said.

Just then, a weasel wiggled into the box—

quick as a wink. A big wolf was after him!

Little  waved her wand. "I wish you would be a good wolf," she said.

She put the wolf into her box with the weasel,
the woodpecker, the wiggly worms, and the
woodchuck. Now the box was full.

Little  found a wheelbarrow.

"Whee!" she said. "This is just

what I need."

She wheeled the wheelbarrow. Away they

went, along a winding road to the water.

"Let's wade in the water," she said.

But the wolf, weasel, woodpecker, wiggly worms, and woodchuck did not want to wade. They watched.

"Wow!" said a walrus. "You look wacky

to me. You have funny feet."

"You look wacky to me," said Little .

"You have funny whiskers."

Little  put the walrus into the box.

The walrus winked at the wolf.

Little  went back to the water. The wind blew the waves up and down.

Then she saw a big whale. The whale whistled.

"I wish I could put the whale in my box, but it is

too big," she said.

Little  waved her wand and found a big

wagon. It was big enough for a whale!

She put everything into the wagon and walked by a wall. What was behind the wall? Watermelons!

"Whoopee!" whooped the woodpeckers

when they saw the watermelons.

"Let's have a watermelon party," said Little .

And they did.

Little 's Word List

wagon

wall

walrus

wand

water

watermelon

wave

weasel

well

whale

wheelbarrow

whiskers

wind

wishing well

wolf

wood chips

woodchuck

woodpecker

woods

worm

Other Words with Little

waffle

waterfall

wig

wallet

web

windmill

walnut

wheel

window

wasp

wheelchair

wing

watch

whistle

woman

More to Do!

Little **W** found many **W** things on her walk. Here's a silly rhyming **W** word game you can play on your own or with friends.

Directions:

Repeat the first three lines of the verse below. For the last line, fill in your own **W** word and silly ending to the sentence.

Rhyming:

We went walking. Wild, wild walking.
We walked high, we walked low.
We walked some more, and what do you know?
We saw waffles! Wiggly wiggly waffles. Yum!

We went walking. Wild, wild walking.
We walked high, we walked low.
We walked some more, and what do you know?
We saw wheels! Big round wheels. Wheeeeee!

Your Turn!

Here are some words
to help you get started:

- waiter
- wax
- weeds
- wheat
- wire
- wrappers
- wren

Harris County Public Library
Houston, Texas

About the Author

Best-selling author Jane Belk Moncure (1926–2013) wrote more than 300 books throughout her teaching and writing career. After earning a master's degree in early childhood education from Columbia University, she became one of the pioneers in that field. In 1956, she helped form the Virginia Association for Early Childhood Education, which established the first statewide standards for teachers of young children.

Inspired by her work in the classroom, Mrs. Moncure's books became standards in primary education, and her name was recognized across the country. Her success was reflected not only in her books' popularity with parents, children, and educators, but also by numerous awards, including the 1984 C. S. Lewis Gold Medal Award.

About the Illustrator

Rebecca Thornburgh lives in a pleasantly spooky old house in Philadelphia. If she's not at her drawing table, she's reading—or singing with her band, called Reckless Amateurs. Rebecca has one husband, two daughters, and two silly dogs.